The GOOD Luck Glasses

by Sara London

Illustrated by Jacqueline Rogers

Hello Reader! — Level 3

SCHOLASTIC INC.

Cartwheel
·B·O·O·K·S·®

New York   Toronto   London   Auckland   Sydney   Mexico City   New Delhi   Hong Kong

Chapter One

Nomi Miller had just turned seven. Seven seemed like a perfect number to Nomi. It was easy to remember.

Hello, Family Members,

Learning to read is one of the most important accomplishments of early childhood. **Hello Reader!** books are designed to help children become skilled readers who like to read. Beginning readers learn to read by remembering frequently used words like "the," "is," and "and"; by using phonics skills to decode new words; and by interpreting picture and text clues. These books provide both the stories children enjoy and the structure they need to read fluently and independently. Here are suggestions for helping your child *before*, *during*, and *after* reading:

Before
- Look at the cover and pictures and have your child predict what the story is about.
- Read the story to your child.
- Encourage your child to chime in with familiar words and phrases.
- Echo read with your child by reading a line first and having your child read it after you do.

During
- Have your child think about a word he or she does not recognize right away. Provide hints such as "Let's see if we know the sounds" and "Have we read other words like this one?"
- Encourage your child to use phonics skills to sound out new words.
- Provide the word for your child when more assistance is needed so that he or she does not struggle and the experience of reading with you is a positive one.
- Encourage your child to have fun by reading with a lot of expression . . . like an actor!

After
- Have your child keep lists of interesting and favorite words.
- Encourage your child to read the books over and over again. Have him or her read to brothers, sisters, grandparents, and even teddy bears. Repeated readings develop confidence in young readers.
- Talk about the stories. Ask and answer questions. Share ideas about the funniest and most interesting characters and events in the stories.

I do hope that you and your child enjoy this book.

—Francie Alexander
Reading Specialist,
Scholastic's Learning Ventures

For Dinah and Ilana,
my first nieces and first-class
research assistants.
And for Dean and his always
excellent eye.
—S.L.

Special thanks to
Dr. Neal Kramer, O.D., for all
your help with this book.
—J.R.

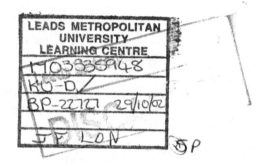
Text copyright © 2000 by Sara London.
Illustrations copyright © 2000 by Jacqueline Rogers.
All rights reserved. Published by Scholastic Inc.
SCHOLASTIC, HELLO READER, CARTWHEEL BOOKS and associated logos
are trademarks and/or registered trademarks of Scholastic Inc.

Library of Congress Cataloging-in-Publication Data
London, Sara.
    Good luck glasses / by Sara London; illustrated by Jacqueline Rogers.
    p. cm. — (Hello reader! Level 3)
    "Cartwheel books."
    Summary: Seven-year-old Nomi decides that she is lucky when the new glasses
she gets help her see things more clearly.
    ISBN 0-590-97212-X
    [1. Eyeglasses Fiction.] I. Rogers, Jacqueline, ill. II. Title. III. Series.
PZ7.L8435Go 2000
[E]—dc21   99-29207
                                                                      CIP
                                                                       AC
10 9 8 7 6 5 4   02 03 04

Printed in the U.S.A.   24
First printing, February 2000

Mom

Dad

Nomi

Gabriel

Lilly

There were seven days in the week.
She lived at number 7 Duncan Lane.
And there were seven people in her
family—including Boo the turtle and
Rosenthal the cat, of course.

She had blown out eight candles on her cake. But one had been for good luck.

"What kind of good luck?" Nomi asked her father.

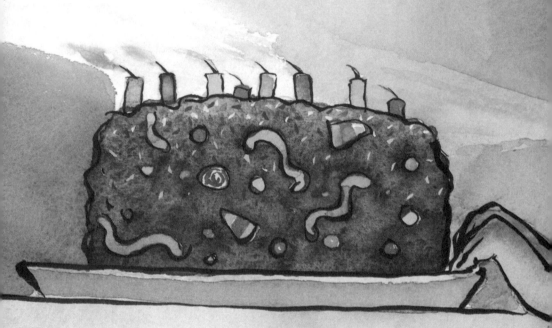

"Well," said her father, "something special that will happen just to you."

Nomi wondered what special thing would happen.

Before long, something did begin to happen. But it didn't seem like good luck.

"What do you see here?" Nomi's teacher asked one day. Mrs. Lacy was pointing to the chalkboard.

"A lot of little dancers in a parade?" said Nomi. "In the snow?" she added.

"Snow?" said Mrs. Lacy. "Oh dear!"

All the children laughed. Nomi laughed, too, but she wasn't sure what was so funny.

"These are words, not snow," said Mrs. Lacy.

tree   house
three   horse

"Oh," said Nomi. But she was embarrassed now. She thought she should say something to explain.

"Well, sometimes words look like alphabet soup," she said.

The children laughed even harder this time.

At dinner that night, Gabriel looked at Nomi across the table.

"Stop squinting at me!" he said.

"I'm not!" said Nomi. "Anyway, it makes you look less like a clown when I do!"

"Enough!" said their father. "Nomi, there will be no more squinting."

Nomi looked at her mother, whose face was as blurry as an angel's.

Then one day Nomi tripped over
Rosenthal. Rosenthal was not very
happy about having his tail stepped on.

"All I saw was a sneaky shadow,"
Nomi told her mother. Even Boo had
begun to look like a little green blob.

"Nomi," said her mother, "I think it's
time to see the eye doctor."

Chapter Two

Nomi's mother and father took her to Dr. Minsky's office. Nomi sat in a big blue chair. Dr. Minsky put his foot on a pedal and the chair rose higher and higher.

"I'm going to turn the lights out for just a minute," said Dr. Minsky.

He turned on a projector. A picture appeared on the wall.

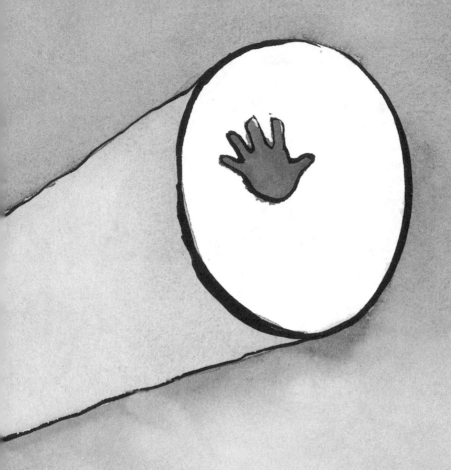

"What do you see?" he asked.

"A porcupine?" said Nomi.

"Well, a birthday cake sometimes looks like a porcupine," said Dr. Minsky. "What do you see now?" he asked, changing the picture.

"Um," said Nomi, "a chicken?"

"I suppose a hand can look like a chicken," he said. He made the pictures red, then green.

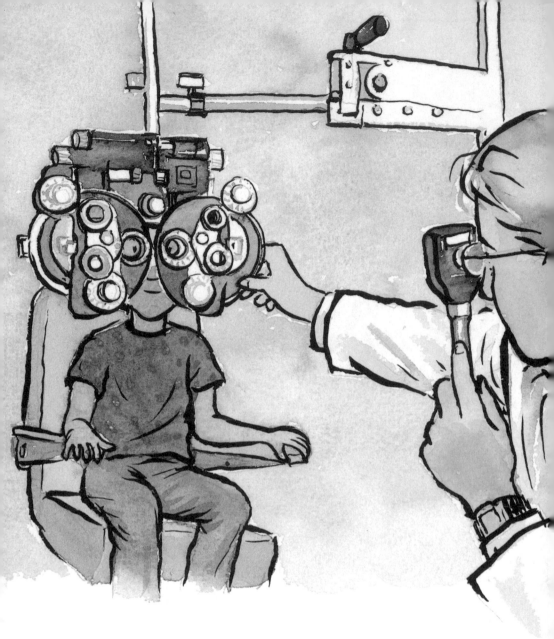

Then Nomi looked through a machine with two eye holes. At first everything looked blurry. Dr. Minsky switched the lenses back and forth.

"Wow! Everything looks so clear now," Nomi said finally.

"I'm going to shine a little flashlight into your eyes now," said Dr. Minsky. "It won't hurt at all."

He asked her to look up and down and to the side. "In your eyes I see beautiful little trees," he told her.

"Trees?" said Nomi. "How can I have trees in my eyes?"

"They're veins that carry blood through your eyes," explained Dr. Minsky. "They look like winter branches with no leaves on them."

When the exam was over, Dr. Minsky stood up.

"Well, you're in luck now. I think I can help you," he said.

Luck. There's that word again, thought Nomi. *Something special must be going on.*

"Do letters ever look like little dancing sticks?" Dr. Minsky asked.

"They do!" said Nomi. "They really do!"

"Do you ever do this to see better?" asked Dr. Minsky. He squinted his eyes at Nomi.

She looked at her mother and father.

"Sometimes," she said.

"Well, young lady," said Dr. Minsky. "It looks like you're going to need glasses."

"I am?" asked Nomi.

Nomi's father raised his eyebrows above the rims of his own glasses.

"That must be my luck!" said Nomi.

Dr. Minsky and Nomi's mother and father all looked at one another.

"Tomorrow we'll shop for glasses," said Nomi's mother.

Chapter Three

Gabriel and Lilly wanted to help Nomi pick out her glasses. So the whole family climbed into the car. Boo didn't even come out of his shell, but Rosenthal sat in the window and watched them drive away.

At the optometrist's office, Nomi tried on many pairs of glasses.

One funny pair was shaped like stop signs.

Another pair was way too big.

Another pair was way too small.

Some made her look awfully silly.

But the candy-striped ones were the best.

Then Nomi's mother found an orange pair. Orange was Nomi's favorite color.

It was going to be hard to choose. Looking at so many glasses made Nomi feel tired, even sort of dizzy—like a dancer in a crazy snow parade!

Finally, Nomi's mother said the orange ones definitely made her look very grown up.

Gabriel said they were very bright.

Little Lilly said, "Fruit!"

house

horse

One week later, Nomi had new orange glasses. *These feel kind of funny on my face*, she thought. *But everything looks so much clearer.*

The writing on the board at school looked like writing! HOUSE looked like HOUSE and HORSE looked like HORSE.

All the children at school wanted to hear about her new glasses. Nomi felt proud as she explained about the tests at the doctor's office, and the veins that looked like trees.

"But finding the right pair of glasses was the trickiest part of all," she said.

Chapter Four

Gabriel and Lilly wanted glasses now, too. *They always want everything I have,* thought Nomi.

"When you grow up, you'll get lucky, too," she told them.

Good luck was being able to see better than ever, she told Gabriel and Lilly.

Bad luck was being unable to read the chalkboard at school and tripping over Rosenthal.

Rosenthal was still afraid he'd get stepped on, though. He watched Nomi from a safe spot behind a chair. But Boo came out of his shell to see her new glasses.

Every morning now, as soon as Nomi
got out of bed, she put on her new
glasses and wore them all day long.
    At night she cleaned them with a
special fluid, and put them in a case
with flowers on it.

One night Nomi dreamed that everyone in her family—even Boo and Rosenthal—had new glasses.

"What if my crazy dream came true?" said Nomi at breakfast.

"That would be just our luck," said Nomi's mother.

"I think two of us with glasses are enough," said Nomi's father. "We're the lucky ones."

And Nomi did, indeed, feel very lucky. Now everything looked much clearer, much brighter, and much more beautiful than ever before.

Letters looked like letters, words looked like words, Boo looked like Boo.

And Rosenthal? Well, Rosenthal didn't look like a sneaky shadow anymore.

He looked like Rosenthal!